Gullywasher Gulch

by Marianne Mitchell
Illustrated by Normand Chartier

Marianne Mitchell

A raining day story for you, RJ

BOYDS MILLS PRESS

Published by Boyds Mills Press, Inc.
A Highlights Company
815 Church Street
Honesdale, Pennsylvania 18431
Printed in China
Visit our Web site at www.boydsmillspress.com

Publisher Cataloging-in-Publication Data

Mitchell, Marianne.
Gullywasher gulch / by Marianne Mitchell ; illustrated by Normand Chartier. —1st ed.
[32] p. : col. ill. ; cm.
Summary: Ebenezer Overall's collection of nails, shingles, lumber, and other "useless junk" comes in mighty handy
when a gullywasher of a rainstorm destroys the town of Dry Gulch.
ISBN 1-56397-123-2
1. Rain and rainfall Fiction — Juvenile literature. 2. Building materials —
Collectors and collecting — Fiction — Juvenile literature. (1. Rain and rainfall — Fiction.
2. Building materials — Collectors and collecting — Fiction.)
I. Chartier, Normand. II. Title.
[E] 21 AC CIP 2002
2001096391

First edition, 2002
The text of this book is set in 15-point Stone Serif.

10 9 8 7 6 5 4 3 2

To Jim
—M. M.

For Uncle Wayne and
Uncle Jim's rainy day
—N. C.

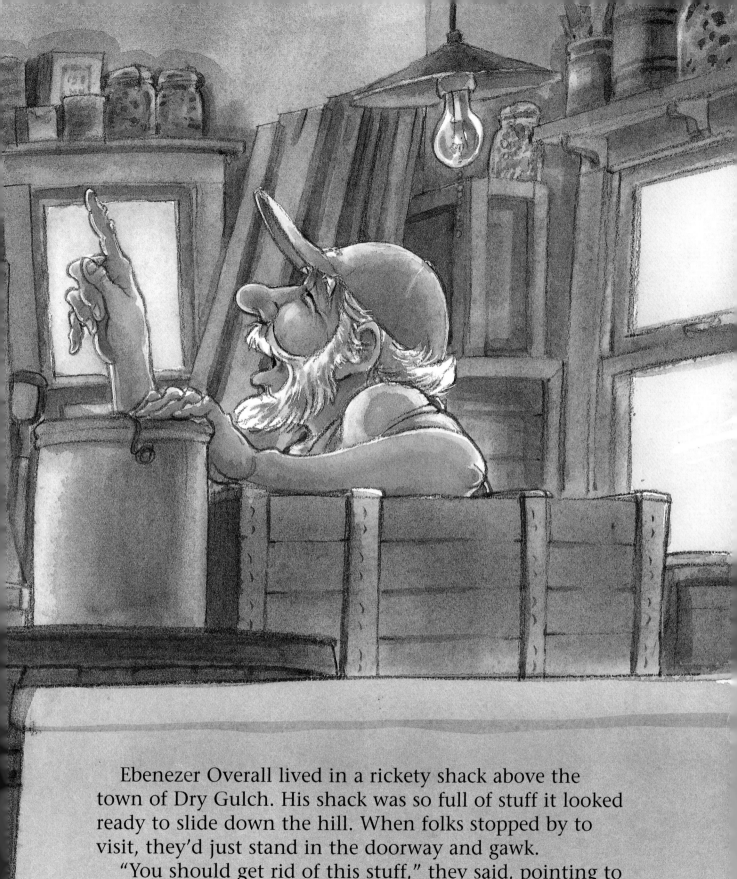

Ebenezer Overall lived in a rickety shack above the town of Dry Gulch. His shack was so full of stuff it looked ready to slide down the hill. When folks stopped by to visit, they'd just stand in the doorway and gawk.

"You should get rid of this stuff," they said, pointing to the barrels of nails, tools, beans, and crockery.

But old Eb shook his head. "Nope. I'm savin' up for a rainy day. You never know when it'll come in handy."

Eb's yard was just as crowded. In between piles of lumber, stacks of shingles, and bundles of tarpaper, Eb grew five kinds of beans in a little garden. Come fall, he'd harvest them, dry them out, and pour them into another barrel.

When his sister Ella May came to visit she'd say, "Ebenezer Overall, you're just an old pack rat. Why in tarnation do you need all this stuff?"

"I'm savin' it for a rainy day," Eb would answer. "You never know what'll happen."

When Eb wasn't growing beans or saving nails, he did a little prospecting. For nearly fifty years, he'd hiked the rugged mountains behind his shack, looking for gold. The townsfolk figured he'd found some, too—a strike worth millions.

"Wish he'd tell us where the gold is," Mayor Dan grumbled. "We could all use a few nuggets."

But old Eb kept quiet. Whenever he came back from the mountains with shiny gold nuggets in his pocket, he'd wait until dark and dig a little hole. Then he'd reach down, drop in a pouch full of gold, and pat the sand over the hole.

"You stay put now. Some rainy day I'll be needin' ya." But since rain was as scarce as a jackalope, he figured that'd be a while.

That summer it was so dry the sun came up as a big ball of dust.

It was so hot that the lizards hobbled around on stick crutches, so they wouldn't burn their scaly toes.

Why, it was so hot that when Eb made his breakfast, he just set his coffeepot in the sun and waited for the water to boil. The coffee went down real good with his rock-fried eggs and his sand-warmed beans.

One sizzly morning, Eb decided to go prospecting. He packed up his burro and headed for the hills. He noticed the air had a mighty peculiar scent to it—real spicy-like. But he paid it no mind and set about digging up more nuggets.

About midday, a rumble in the sky made him look up. Dark clouds billowed overhead. Lightning flashed and then, *Ker-RACK!*

"Well, it's about time!" cried Eb. He grabbed his shovel and burro and hightailed it back to his shack, while fat raindrops splattered in the dust.

"Hope it's not one of them skittery storms," he muttered to his burro. "The kind that spits a few drops and then disappears."

But this cloud looked like it might want to set a spell, and so it did. The rain came down like someone had unzipped a heavenly ocean. The thirsty ground and plants slurped up every drop.

Eb sat in his shack, watching
and worrying. He knew the desert
couldn't handle too much rain all at once.
He kept his eye on the nearby gully. It was
normally a dry wash, but now it churned with
gushy brown water. Soon a tumbling torrent
came roaring straight toward Eb's shack.

First the old shack trembled. Then it shook. Then it splintered. *SWOOSH!* That gullywasher carried Eb and all his stuff right down the hillside toward town. Clinging to his burro, he rode those rapids like a rodeo cowboy.

By the time the rain stopped, the town was a shambles. Every building had washed away. Folks had grabbed on to any old post, hanging on for dear life. Now they looked a lot like mud-covered stick lizards on a hot summer day.

"We're ruined!" sighed Mayor Dan.
"What'll we do?" cried Sheriff Amos.
"What's this?" asked little Miranda, opening her fist.
"I found it in the mud. Is it gold?"

The mere whisper of gold set everyone to work, cleaning and scraping off mud. When they were done, they'd found gold nuggets all over. The big round lumps in the middle of the street turned out to be barrels of nails, tools, beans, and crockery. The square lumps were bundles of wood, tarpaper, and shingles.

"But it all belongs to Eb," said little Miranda. "Can we use it?"

A hush fell over the crowd. Every face turned toward Ebenezer Overall.

"Sure as shootin'!" said Eb. "We'll build us a new town, and we'll call it Gullywasher Gulch."

"We're saved!" said Mayor Dan.

"It's a miracle!" said Preacher Stan.

"It's what I've been tellin' ya," said Eb.
"I was savin' it all for a rainy gullywasher day,
just like this."